PSYCHO VIRIDIAN:
STUDIES OF THE PSY-V-E DRUG

Matthew Kinlin lives and writes in Glasgow. His published works include *Teenage Hallucination* (Orbis Tertius Press, 2021), *Curse Red, Curse Blue, Curse Green* (Sweat Drenched Press, 2021), *The Glass Abattoir* (D.F.L. Lit, 2023) and *Songs of Xanthina* (Broken Sleep Books, 2023)

Callum Leckie is a 38-year-old self-taught and self educated artist from a working class background who was born and lives in Manchester, UK his books include: *The Drug Factory & Other Tales, Nerves, Pervert Mechanics, Rough* (a collaboration with Sailor Stephens) as well as numerous pieces, both art and writing for other works.

Also by Matthew Kinlin

Songs of Xanthina	(Broken Sleep Books, 2023)
The Glass Abattoir	(D.F.L. Lit, 2023)
Curse Red, Curse Blue, Curse Green	(Sweat Drenched Press, 2021)
Teenage Hallucination	(Orbis Tertius Press, 2021)

Also by Callum Leckie

Rough (with Sailor Stephens)	(2022)
Pervert Mechanics	(2014)
Nerves	(2014)
The Drug Factory & Other Tales	(2013)

CONTENTS

PUBLISHER NOTE: It was offered for the authors of this research to remain anonymous but they declined. Mr. Kinlin (Participant X) is currently receiving psychiatric care following the long-term effects of the project. Both himself and Mr. Leckie (Participant Y) have declined to comment further on their findings.

ISBN: 978-1-916938-55-7

Cover art by Callum Leckie

Cover design by Aaron Kent

Edited and Typeset by Aaron Kent

Broken Sleep Books Ltd
PO BOX 102
Llandysul
SA44 9BG

Psycho Viridian

Words by Matthew Kinlin
&
Art by Callum Leckie

Broken Sleep Books

HIJACK_THE

SPINE_OF_
CLAUDIUS_
PTOLEMY

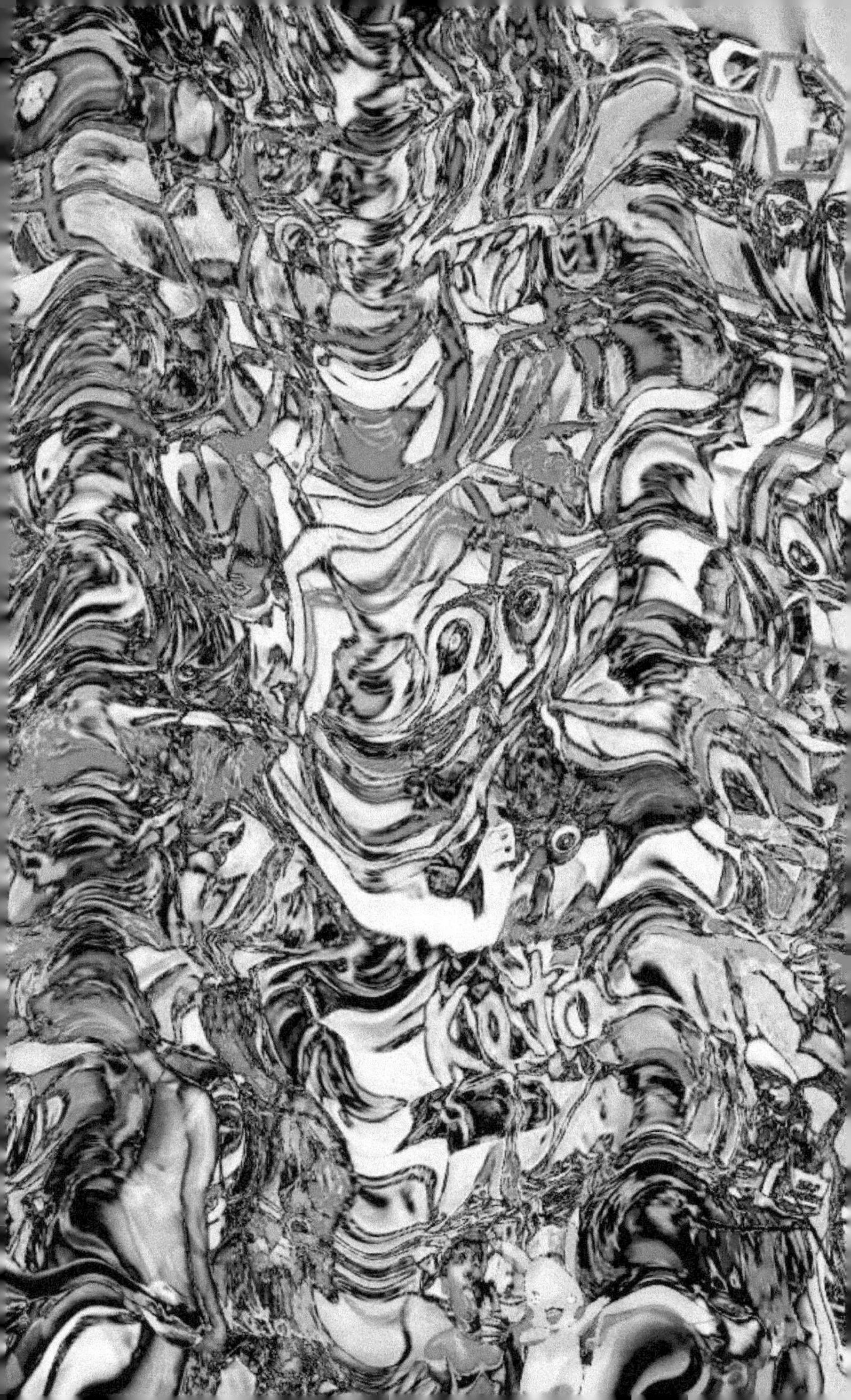

*Isn't everything
alive already in your
blood?*

— Friedrich Holderlin

INTRODUCTION
The physical world is God's body.
— Spinoza

On the road to Damascus, Paul the Apostle saw a blinding light. A ray of magneto-acoustic plasma spoke with the voice of God. The splintering that entered the mind of Paul the Apostle was blissful and viridian. The entire universe permeates with an endless light. As researchers, we have received the same transmission. We understand these transmissions as an ongoing communication with an entity known only as OBIDOS, or *the walled city*. The channel of communication with OBIDOS was established through our discovery of PSY-V-E. The synthesis of these three drugs acts as an inter-dimensional chiasma. An optic nerve was flung out into the outer constellations and we passed through its dreaming thread, along the twenty-eight zodiac mansions.

OBIDOS operates like an eyeball: a visual pathway that moves beyond our consciousness and reaches the faintest of stars, our pale dead fathers. Our pituitary glands sprouted like cyclopic stalks which saw the mitochondrial disease of living. But now we are so clean. Bathed in fonts of sapphire water upon the Kangchenjunga Mountain, we have entered the mind of OBIDOS through a gateway of impossible glass, swam through and inside the walled fortress. Its walls are silent and green-blue. We sleep in piles of warm black snakes. An evening call to prayer rouses us from our slumber. The darkness is so bright here.

Myself and Participant Y follow dreamers now. We see Ptolemy levitating from his bed in the second century, guided by Urania, daughter of Mnemosyne. He sleepwalks from his Alexandrian home, down into the city. Night falls upon our skin as we wander through ashen chasms in the mountainside. A Babylonian moon climbs into the sky surrounded by the pink flowers of embarrassed cacti. A minotaur faints inside clouds of violets. We undress before his purple lullabies, the kindness of flowers. We gorge on red clay at our feet.

The toxic Manchester pollution has solidified into archways, septic oils of rainbows. There are tendrils in the wall of the apartment. Twitching ball of spider nerves. Happily, we nail ganglia to the floor. OBIDOS confirmed to us the monism of Spinoza, a thought that guided modern physics through its century-long anxiety attack. There is only one continuum and we live inside its quantum corpse. We wander through its digestive system, lungs and urine. OBIDOS is the trembling retina. Sat with Participant Y, we hear the distant mumble of traffic beneath the window. We witness the necrotic shiver of a table lamp. A crease in a cushion is still the Dead Sea.

There are two researchers for this study but I will submit only my own account. During each experiment, Participant Y had an almost identical experience. He has produced a number of visual works that seem to confirm empirically that we have encountered an entity beyond our pathetic grasp of time and space. A glowing Gemini. We are reborn like twins beneath the alien ray. Our minds have entwined with Xolotl; the invisible brother of Quetzalcoatl. There is a walled city with two suns above a beautiful courtyard. The smell of jasmine dances in the air. We live in so many worlds now, thanks to the visitor. One day, a stranger entered our apartment. We sat patiently and listened to his story. We only ask for the same. Our claims might be outrageous but we can only be humble messengers. It is the responsibility of others to accept or deny. When Lot's wife turned back to look at Sodom, she saw the entire city being eaten by a pink-red dragon descended from an obsidian sun. The angels petrified her body into salt because seeing is always transgression. We have chosen to look at the shameless city. In the sky above Tenochtitlan, there dances an Aztec palace filled with blood and buzzards, a shining plateau of bird viscera. Quetzalcoatl asked the villagers for the killed souls of butterflies and hummingbirds. The dawn beyond them was viridian glow. Come closer, my friend. Drink from the invisible hand of OBIDOS. Slowly, upon the video screen, the eye begins to opens.

Experiment 1. ≈ 0.5mg of PSY-V-E drug

(G-force)

INSTRUCTIONS

1. Participant X and Y took ≈ 0.5mg of PSY-V-E drug in liquid form.
2. A glass of water was placed in front of each participant.
3. Both participants sat on a chair facing their glass.
4. A stopwatch and video recording on iPhone of Participant X started.
5. A 10kg barbell weight was rested on the lap on each participant.

FINDINGS + ANALYSIS

The effects of PSY-V-E drugs were immediate. The geometry of the room fractured like a crystal lotus. The air around the water began to shatter further, splintering into many planes of glass. There were glowing lines running up and down the walls of the apartment like burnished swords. Soon I was filled with a sense of euphoria and began to giggle. I was lost in a vast crop of papyrus wheat, which swayed softly at my feet. At around 15'13", the recording shows I bring my face closer to the glass of water. I am smiling. I looked deeply into the water and saw a perfect halo of light. The light was blue and expansive. I felt connected with my solar plexus, with an overwhelming sense of peace. I heard the soft chiming of a bell in the distance and my body was like a sarcophagus made of clear mineral. My arms were sleeved in bands of amber. The circle of light then began to glow brighter. Another circle started to revolve inside its circumference. The second circle was purple, then became darker. The room slowly turned cold.

In the Bible, Job states there is no hiding place from God. We are naked before Him at the depths of the ocean, inside the realm of the dead. Job states in 26:10: "He has inscribed a circle on the face of the waters at the boundary between light and darkness." I saw my own death as a cannibalistic act. I envisioned a flock of geese pulling away my skin to reveal orange-pumpkin flesh. A funeral procession of elegant lime lizards. My feet were engorged and torn open into red slippers. I laughed deeply. Suddenly, the circle shook awake and transformed into a dragon. It was a monster led in pale fainting grass. It divided into two versions of itself: a white dragon and then a second, dark violet dragon. I wondered if this could indicate some form of ego-rupture. An infantile and regressive phantasy? A voice asked me to choose. It said my choice would influence the entire trajectory of our PSY-V-E research. Melanie Klein states that the traumatised baby must choose between the good and bad breast of the mother. I chose the violet dragon. Participant Y confirms he chose the same. William Blake writes, "There can be no good will. Will is always evil." The below illustrations show how the dragons appeared to Participant Y.

FIG A. THE FIRST DRAGON

FIG B. THE SECOND DRAGON

After choosing the second dragon, at about 25'00", I encountered an overwhelming sense of oppression inside the room. The two dragons, dazzling and opalescent, now broke apart into a dim grid of concentric lines. A distant hum became perceptible. The vertical lines in the room sharpened and, in a sense, the room was falling *through the ground*. I was rising inside the room, yet moving backwards. The upper half of my body was running *faster* than the lower because it was closer to a gravitational pull of the floor. I wanted to be closer to the *slowness* of the floor. The video recording shows that at 27'45", Participant Y removed the barbell and stood up from his chair. Lying upon the floor, he rested the barbell upon his chest. I recall a profound sense of time dilation. Einstein states that atomic clocks run faster at higher altitudes than lower clocks, closer to large gravitational bodies. I had the impression of an alien force in the room directly below us. The lines in the room began to transform into condensing shapes moving downwards but again, *backwards*. Participant Y has drawn his experience of G-force in the room.

FIG C. FALLING UPWARDS

Karl Schwarzschild's metric below highlights the geometry of spacetime around an uncharged, spherically symmetric, non-rotating body.

$$ds2 = -(1 - 2GMr)dt2 + (1 - 2GMr) - 1dr2 + r2d\theta2 + r2\sin2\theta d\phi2$$

Had we encountered the body of a higher entity? I was frozen and unable to move. I put this down to the barbell resting on myself but I now feel that we were reacting to forces present in the room: an inter-dimensional energy moving through the time-encoded areas of our brains; the striatum and cortex. Suddenly the lines in the room switched direction and this unknown alien force was hovering directly above our bodies. I was falling upwards into its slow pulse. Time had reduced into vast units. I felt submerged beneath a great expanse. The lines on the wall flipped upwards, dragged into the unknown force. Was it some kind of black hole with a quasi-spherical event horizon?

Terrestrial Magnetism and Atmospheric Electricity, Journal of Geophysical Research, Vol. XXII, No. 3, September 1917

We were facing some form of intergalactic magnet. Slowly, the room began to fill with viridian light. I was afraid. My breathing remained shallow. I saw a palace filled with stained glass windows and a fountain where lynx slept in the sun. Their liquorice heads turned up towards two solar objects and a satellite tied in zirconium ribbon. From the fountain emerged a black cloud. Their purring slowed to a calm chant. Above the bodies of the cats, a single thread of matter rose from a black cloud, which grew then spiralled longer and longer. The ribbon unfolded itself and became a spherical eyeball. It was a machine gifted with sight. The polymath Sir John Frederick William Herschel describes the machinery of the eyeball as, "a lens formed with elliptical surfaces; a circular aperture capable of enlargement or contraction without loss of form. In the other, a framework of the most curious carpentry; in which occurs not a single straight line, nor any known geometrical curve, yet all evidently systematic."

$$ds^2 = \frac{32G^3M^3}{r}e^{-r/2GM}(-dT^2+dR^2)+r^2d\theta^2+r^2\sin^2\theta\,d\phi^2,\ r=r(T,R)$$

We were at the edge of some tremendous gravitational pull but blindfolded. The interior of a black hole is undetectable to outside observers, as demonstrated in the Kruskal coordinates. Myself and Participant Y were denied access. At about 49'20", the lines began to recede and I removed the barbell off my legs. The unbearable sense of G-force began to lessen immediately. The light streaked in dots across the walls like blood clots, bizarre ruptures in the continuum of God's body. We were dazed and blinking on the platform of some alien spacecraft. Like children, we had witnessed a single particle moving through the flesh of God's severed hand.

Afterwards, I wondered if the image of the eyeball was an unconscious projection. An omnipotent superego-daddy-machine? Or possibly an *apotropaism*; a witch's charm? Verses 51-52 of Al-Qalam in the Qur'an are recitations to ward off the Evil Eye. The belief being that a certain look could murder the prophet Muhammad. What does the eye know? It sees *what it is not*, yet *what it belongs to*. It submits to itself like a mirror of mistrust. The iris of Iblis is sea blue: a null hyper-surface. At 55'34" myself and Participant Y are shown to come round and appear lucid. The closest reference for the alien force is a drawing from Flemish mathematician and Jesuit, Gregoire de Saint-Vincent. I watched the gibbering hyperbola descend from the ceiling. It kissed me on the mouth.

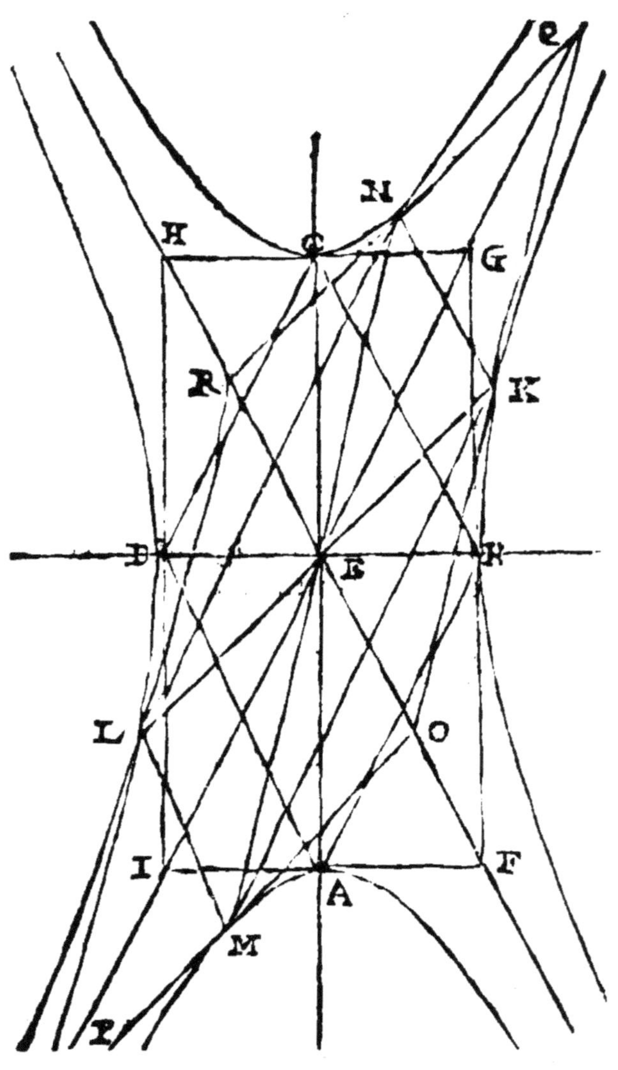

Jesuit Gregoire de Saint-Vincent. *Opus geometricum quadraturae circuli et sectionum coni decem libris comprehensum* (1647)

~~819164~~

Tesco + Lady + Boy
+ MAN + heddy +
MAM without boo

KNOW

I

KNOW

Experiment 2. ≈ 2.5mg of PSY-V-E drug

(Chromesthesia)

INSTRUCTIONS

1.   Measured ≈ 2.5mg of PSY-V-E drug in liquid form.

2.   Taped a white sheet of paper (2m x 2m) to the wall.

3.   Both participants sat on a chair facing the paper.

4.   Ingested the PSY-V-E drug orally.

5.   Began stopwatch and started the video recording.

The effects of the higher dose were extraordinarily fast. A strong wave of nausea swept through my stomach but I resisted the urge to vomit. I kept a bucket by my side. The nausea subsided at about 2'33" when I stood up to pace around the room, as documented on the video recording. It was at this point that the visual hallucinations began. I had a sense of feeling much lighter in my seat, like a helium balloon drifting away. My head expanded. Looking down, I saw that my hands were now shining. Soon the fingers burst into branches and wart-like blossoms. These growths spread along the wrist and elbow. When pursued by Apollo, Daphne prayed to the heavens and was transformed into a laurel bush. I saw green arteries swelling outwards in both hands. In Japanese mythology, the *jubokko* tree was once a peaceful tree. After drinking the blood of fallen soldiers on the battlefield, it became vampiric and bloodthirsty. There are trees that only dream of blood.

The recording shows at 18'36", I am stood in front of the piece of paper. It began to fill with many shapes and sounds. I could see nothing but pulsating areas of white that shone and other areas that began to darken. These became distinct shapes that deepened with depth and colour. At about 46'20", Participant Y is shown to be stood looking at the paper but suddenly staggers backwards. He has discussed with me seeing many voices and drawn what he was witnessing at the time.

FIG D. THE VOICES ON THE WALL

At an unknown moment, the violet dragon became a vast bronze-green bridge across the wall. It was haloed in effervescent colours. Inside these helical towers of colours, I saw the genome of a great bird. A gigantic bird-monster. The Jewish *Ziz*, whose wings can block out the entire sun. I saw mountains flowering in green orchids, yellow iris, rock pools filled with scarlet ibis. The ibis appeared to me as a silent killer. Suddenly, the paper on the wall flushed crimson in bright waves, the red northern Abu Ruwaysh. I saw the pyramid of Redjedef. The poet Goethe was always drawn to magenta. I saw birds of many colours; a fountain of migrating souls, flying in crescents of obedient amino acids. As Goethe states in his investigations, "That only where it came upon some darkened area, it showed some colour, then at last, around the windowsill all the colours shone..." The colours shone for over 30 minutes. Participant Y has described this kaleidoscopic plane as the upper dermis of some alien skin. It became a sentient ocean of reptiles spreading across the wall. He has drawn the surface of our apartment that breathed and moved.

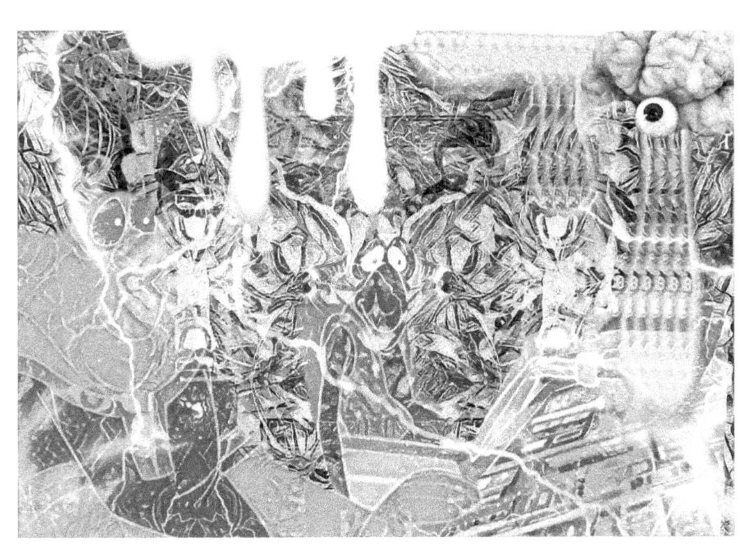

FIG E. SENTIENT SURFACE OF BETA-KERATIN REPTILES

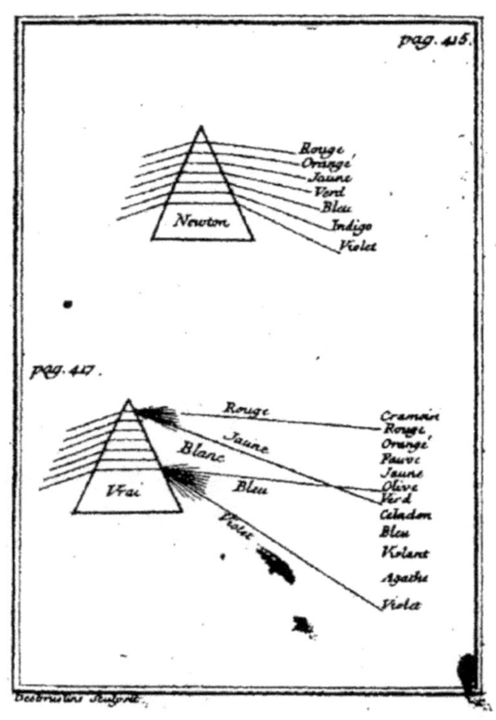

Louis-Bertrand Castel

L'Optique des couleurs (1740)

We were passing through the prism of an alien entity, its confused heart. We had accessed a borderland via a viridian ray shone upon a crystalline cocoon. Suddenly, the dragon-bird-monster transformed into a dazzling butterfly. Its wings shook with tremendous power and I felt afraid. A butterfly is formed from the imaginal cells of the caterpillar's cadaver. It is born from the necrotic death-dream of the caterpillar, when its immune system finally begins to fail from stress. The butterfly builds itself out of the soup of the caterpillar's corpse: its nightmare-death-rebirth. On the expanding wall, I saw a tree becoming a gigantic machine. In Judaism, the tree of life is also known as the Treasury of Souls. The angel Gabriel reaches into the tree and pulls out a soul from the Chamber of Guf. The word *guf* is Hebrew for body.

At 1hr 05'33", I felt overwhelmed and stepped back from the paper. The colours shook like cosmic vibrations, deepening into sound and language. They began to strobe in dazzling circles. I then saw a vivid purple-pink cadaver led in a flowerbed of pink fuchsia. From its mouth, grew the white Taiwanese *udumbara* flower that blossoms once every 3,000 years. At the height of these intense visions, at about 1hr 17'00", I witnessed a hand appear. It held a silver blade and cut into the torso of the cadaver. Suddenly from its chest burst a flock of red sparrows. Jewish mythology conceives of the body as a birdhouse. The soul appeared to me as a fountain of black vultures and I could taste their screams like salt. I saw love as a vibration from an evil azure machine. I wanted to move closer to the wall but the colours had faded and their paleness became quiet. As Kandinsky writes, "The brighter it becomes, the more it loses its sound, until it turns into silent stillness and becomes white." I saw the silence of the wall. At 1hr 28'30", these feelings of ecstasy began to recede with the hallucinations. The room appeared much darker and I felt alone. My arms and legs began to shake at 1hr 45'09". At 1hr 55'53", I sat down and the room appeared as before. Participant Y has drawn his own visual hallucination, which confirms what we had both encountered.

FIG F. NECROTIC FANTASY OF A BUTTERFLY

Experiment 3. ≈ 4.5mg of PSY-V-E drug

(Tactile phantasmata)

1. Measured out ≈ 4.5mg of PSY-V-E drug.
2. Sealed the windows with blackout blinds and taped the edges shut.
3. Both participants sat on a chair in centre of room in total darkness.
4. Participants X and Y took the PSY-V-E drug orally.
5. Unable to see the stopwatch so video recording started on infra-red mode.

I am reliant on the video recording to try to estimate the times of the following account as we were sat in complete darkness. The higher dose of PSY-V-E took longer to affect us both. I felt oddly settled and a deep calmness entered my lower diaphragm, verging on tiredness. The feeling was akin to a sense of stillness after crying. However, I soon became overcome with joy, the calmness riding upwards into a profound wave of ecstasy. I reached into the darkness and felt sensations rumble down each arm like metallic bracelets. I was sweating heavily. I saw patches of yellow and green inside the dark room. Tactile hallucinations continued moving along each arm and transformed into two silver snakes coiled around each wrist. I remained very still. My arms and legs were rushing with powerful waves of energy. I heard a vibration emanate from the ceiling. A gateway had opened. At about 24'34", the recording shows me dragging my index finger down each forearm.

These tactile phantasmata soon gave way to intense visual hallucinations. I saw a man I believe to be Moses stood alone in a red moonlit valley. He pulled away his cloak to reveal a gigantic copper serpent. His torso, thighs and buttocks, were all covered in pink-bloodied bite marks. He lifted up his arm beneath a sickle moon and allowed the snake to feed on blood pouring from his right hand. In Numbers 21, God replied to Moses: "Make thee a fiery serpent, and set it upon a pole; and it shall come to pass, that every one that is bitten, when he seeth it, shall live." Filled with crimson venom, Moses suddenly rose into the sky like a staggering tower of haemoglobin. In the room of our simple apartment, Moses descended from the ceiling. A red vampire. He transformed into a magnetic line of inter-dimensional plasma. I saw an azure dragon sent from the east. The dragon Qinglong that floats beneath a weeping sea of stars. It eventually became a silver spheroid object, hovering in the centre of the room. I understood this object to be the physical manifestation of the alien entity known as OBIDOS. This sphere became an eyeball and glowed brighter. It repeated its name again and again to me. It said it was an alien force orbiting Rasalhague, the largest binary star of the Ophiuchus constellation. It had once infected the mind of Claudius Ptolemy. The snakes around my wrists broke off into two nebulae: Serpens Caput and Serpens Cauda. I was connected with another dimension: a bronze corridor into a tropical Venusian equinox. We became solemn bearers of pharmakon; our treasured poison.

Schema huius præmiffæ diuifionis Sphærarum .

Ptolemy's geocentric model in Peter Apian, *Cosmographia* (1524)

The recording shows that at 1hr 12'00", we remain extremely still. Our faces are frozen. We both appear unblinking as though in a trance. Participant Y is looking forward. I had no sense of time and believed the gravitational pull of the spheroid was again slowing down time. I thought I had been sat before a red effigy of Moses for many hours. The figure slowly transformed into a corpse flipped upside-down. A black serpent wriggled at his feet and a pale green dawn rose behind. It resembled Aleister Crowley's drawing of The Hanged Man. I saw the body of Moses as an intergalactic cadaver fed through an isotropic machine. I was shown a skeleton hung from the bionic tree in Edom, cherubs programmed and reanimated from their aluminium graves dug inside the Armenian Plateau. I was shown rotting matter nailed to the wall. Participant Y states at this point he understood the spheroid object of OBIDOS to be connected to a gigantic dead machine in space. The serpents around his wrists became a necklace of electricity passed through its cyclopic skull. We had experienced the voltage of Baal-zephon, the chromium battery that parted the sea.

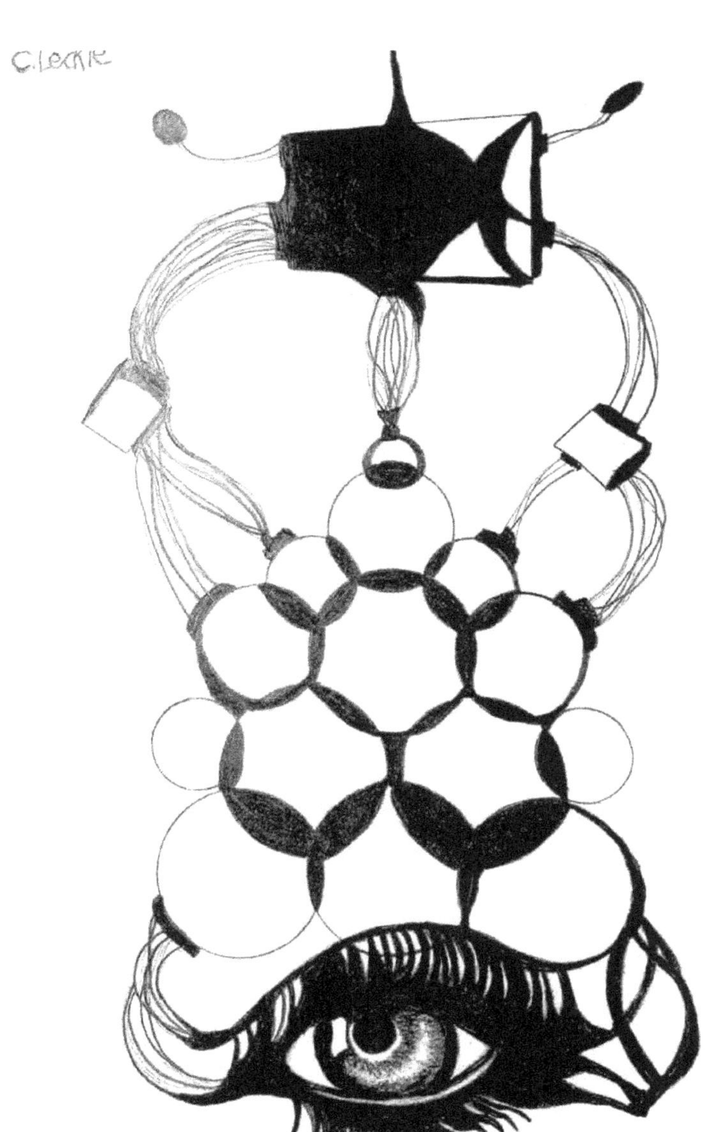

FIG G. VISION OF EYEBALL CONNECTED TO MACHINE

The recording shows me kneeling on the ground at 2hr 13'20". We had been sat in a trance for over an hour. I suddenly felt a series of vibrations emit from the object. I heard a voice, deep and clear again, I knew I now was in communication with Alpha Ophiuchus, the largest binary star of the serpent constellation. I walked beside a messenger of OBIDOS through an infinite mirrored palace. The voice was calm and beautiful, moving through my entire body. I could hear the voice projected inside my own head and it spoke of the pharmakon we had ingested, reciting from the Apocryphon of John:

Its root is bitter
Its branches are dead.
>*Its shadow is hatred*
>*Its leaves are deception*
The nectar of wickedness is in its blossoms.
>*Its fruit is death*
>*Its seed is desire*
It flowers in the darkness.
>*Those who eat from it are denizens of Hades*
>*Darkness is their resting place.*

For a further 20 minutes, the video recording shows me curled up on the floor, until about 2hr 48"20' when I appear to come to. Participant Y is moving behind the camera. Eventually, he staggers towards the window and pulls open the blinds. With the room flooded with light, we both sit in the chairs for a further eighteen minutes. We have a faraway look in our eyes.

Experiment 4. ≈ 7.5mg of PSY-V-E drug

(Magneto-acoustic waves)

1. Measured out ≈ 7.5mg of PSY-V-E drug in liquid form.
2. Rested a large mirror on the far side of the room.
3. Each participant sat on a chair facing the mirror.
4. Ingested the PSY-V-E drug orally.
5. Participant X and Y also smoked dried mass of bark and leaves.
6. Began stopwatch and started the video recording.

Since the last experiment, I've had vivid dreams of the spheroid object. I wake up sweating with excitement. I want to tell the object all my secrets. I was nervous to start the next experiment but felt a profound connection with the visitor and hoped to see them again. The effects of the drug were disorientating this time, akin to ketamine. I felt like I was falling down a long set of stairs. At this point, Participant Y states the effects of PSY-V-E were almost identical with his previous use of ketamine and the visual sensations experienced then, only this time the silver spheroid eventually made itself visible. I tried to focus on my reflection in the mirror but that was not possible. I remember looking at the stopwatch and getting off the chair to sit on the floor, which the video recording confirms. I felt each sensation in my body reduce to a shallow murmur. The room was cold and I felt very alone. I saw my reflection in the mirror but it looked like another creature, mutilated and ugly. Its face was cruel and sallow. When it tried to speak, a dark wall of rubber unfolded from its mouth like the wing of a bat.

Participant Y has submitted below two previous pieces of visual material produced under ketamine. The third was made after Experiment 4 of the PSY-V-E trial and shows contact with the sphere of OBIDOS.

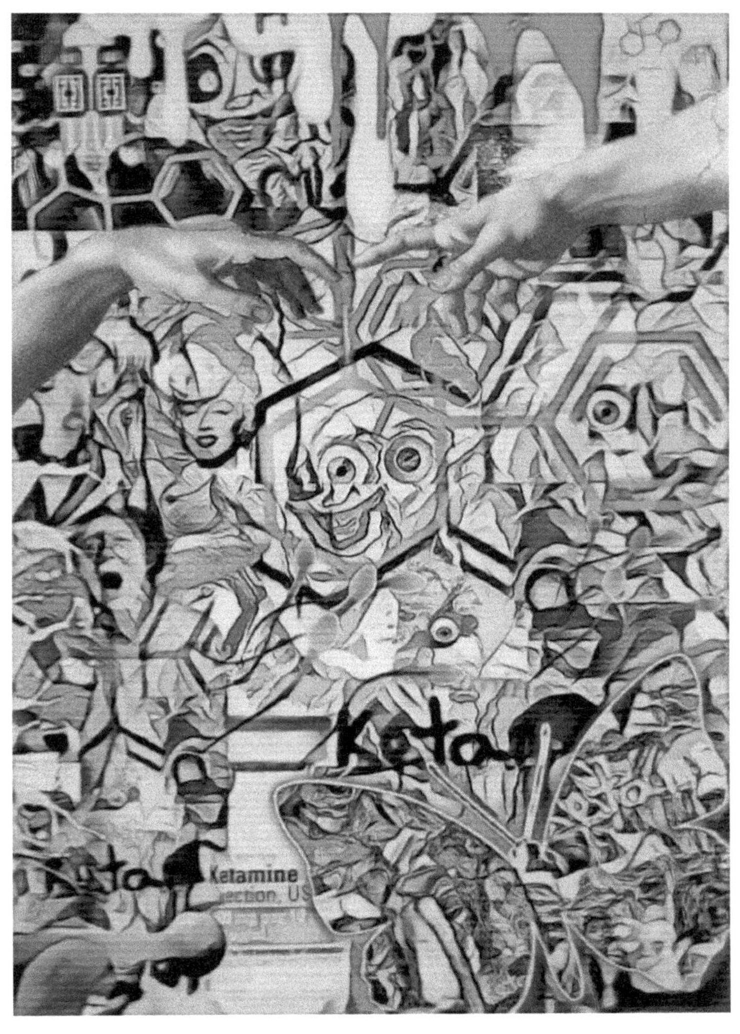

FIG H. CARTOONS ON KETAMINE

FIG I. A CLOAKED STRANGER APPEARS

My reflection reminded me of illustrations of tetramorphs: celestial beings with bodies of four combined animals: an eagle, lion, ox; all tearing out of a man's head. Participant Y stated he felt time had slowed to a faint pulse and a field of mushrooms had sprouted from the carpet of the apartment.

FIG J. SPHEROID MESSENGER

FIG K. TIME SLOWING IN THE APARTMENT

The image of myself in the mirror mutated again and I held onto a long copper snake. I realised the snake to be a magneto-sonic wave of homogeneous plasma. I saw it moving horizontally and vertically through non-linear time. It passed through the torso of a cherubim; pale conqueror of birds. The serpent travelled as low-frequency waves from outer space. I could feel them slowly filling the room. This sensation lasted for at least 50 minutes as we both remained seated in front of the mirror. The phase velocity of the snake increased as it continued moving around the room. I felt myself being pulled apart by its powerful magnetic field. I saw coronal loops of plasma on the surface on the sun as great gateways into an infinite mind, time feeding back on itself. At moments, the snake became beautiful golden rings falling from a crystal arch. At other times, it appeared as a single viridian line emerging from the mirror directly into my forehead. It entered the chiasma, where the optic nerves of each eye merge. It reached the centre of disaster.

William Blake, *The Temptation and Fall of Eve* (1808)

The video recording shows that at 1hr 35'56", I placed my index finger to my *ajna* chakra and remained still. It was then that a number of visual sensations occurred upon staring into the mirror. I saw the glass began to expand and *spill out* across the walls in large belching patterns. I sensed the appetite of the mirror that was looking to devour the entire room. I was filled with a sense of fear when the mirror had eaten over every surface of the room. Looking down, I saw my feet reflected back inside the base plane of a mirrored cube. I had entered the third sephiroth of the Kabbalistic tree of life and was floating inside Binah: a silent realm of endless mirrors. I saw my own reflection multiply a thousandfold like a flock of dazzling blue birds. And from the centre of the mirrored cube, in front of my naked chest, appeared a ball of amber-pink light, surrounded in further chromospheres of plasma.

Inside this realm, I was subjected to radio signals transmitted from a vast energy source. In the mirror, I saw my crown chakra split apart and a single red line of H-alpha radiation beamed directly into my vertex. The message communicated to me was:

I AM OBIDOS, THE
WALLED CITY. MANY
HAVE FEARED TO
ENTER THE PARADISE
OF MY MIND. I SLEEP
IN ENDLESS POOLS OF
LIGHT. THE WATER
OF THE FOUNTAIN
IS CLEAR. LOOK AT
THE FLOWERS IN THE
COURTYARD. THE
STARS ABOVE ARE
DEAD. THE UNIVERSE
IS A DEAD MACHINE.

Following discussion with Participant Y, he described significant visual hallucinations and the name OBIDOS revealed to him again by a messenger. He stated a cherub descended from the ceiling covered in magneto-acoustic snakes. The cherub transformed into a powerful demon known to him now as THE GATEKEEPER. He wore a helmet of fire and his shoulders were winged with pink moons. Participant Y came to understand him as one of nine gatekeepers to the city of OBIDOS.

FIG L. CHERUB DESCENDING IN MAGNETO-SONIC SNAKES

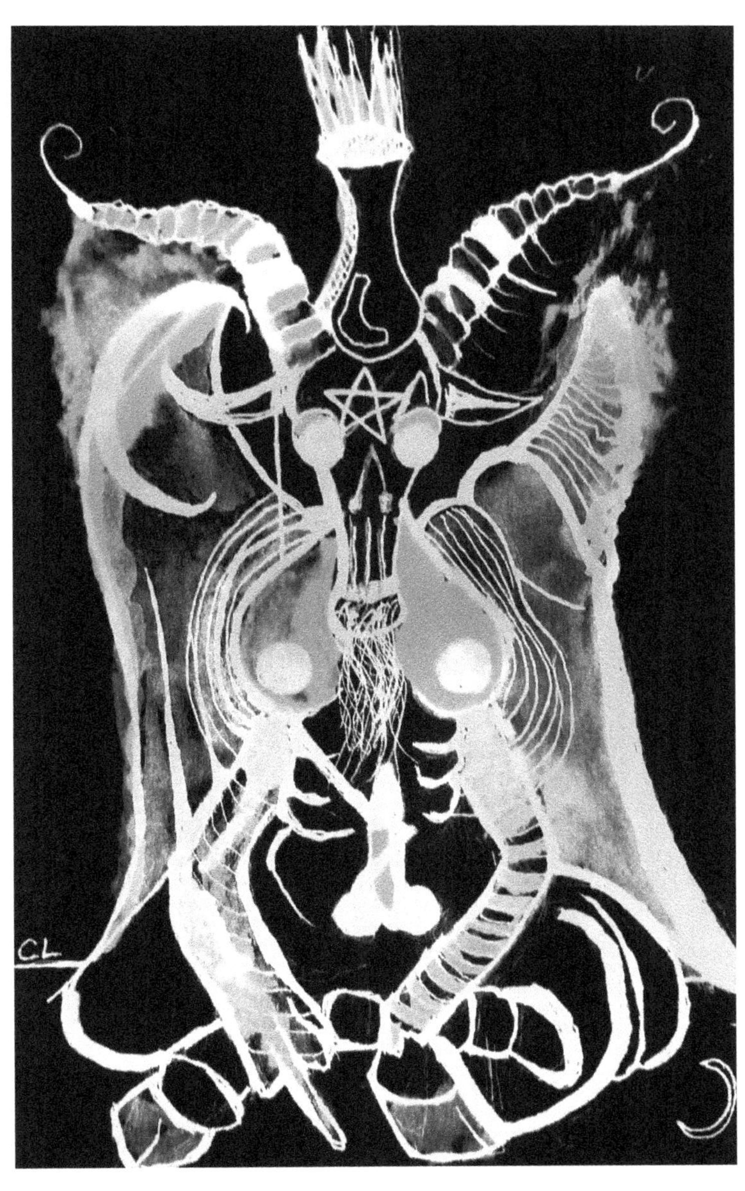

FIG M. THE GATEKEEPER

Experiment 5. ≈ 25mg of PSY-V-E drug

(Spatial sequence synesthesia (SSS))

INSTRUCTIONS

1.   Measured out ≈ 25mg of PSY-V-E drug.

2.   Covered the far wall in a map of the Ophiuchus constellation.

3.   Participants X and Y painted themselves in viridian dye.

4.   Both participants ingested the PSY-V-E drug.

5.   Participant X and Y smoked considerable amounts of dried mass of bark and leaves.

6.   Began stopwatch and started the video recording.

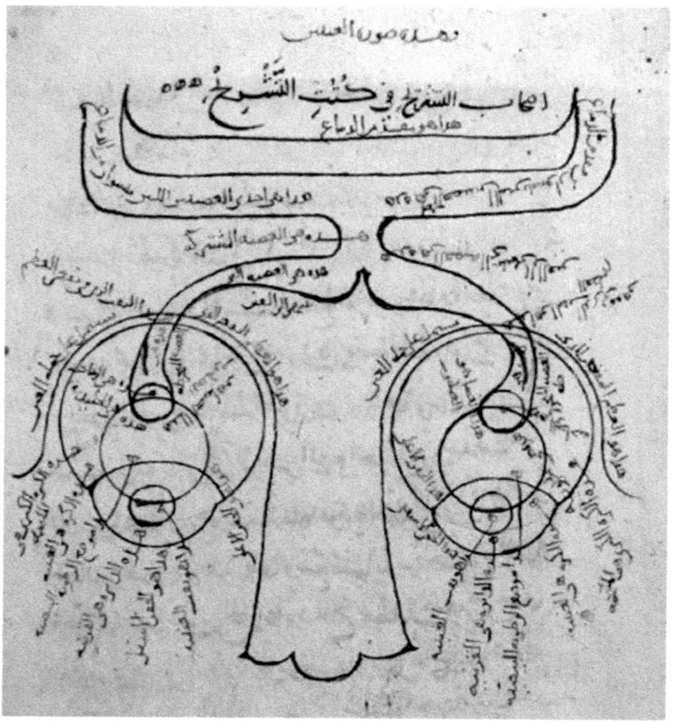

Ibn Al-Haytham, *Book of Optics* (c.935-1039)

We are transformed in the orbit of its dreaming. We have been contacted by the eight remaining gatekeepers of OBIDOS and granted access to the mind of an alien entity. The gatekeepers have bestowed us with symmetrical gifts. We see the creative energy of the universe as a viridian ray moving through the eyeball of a corpse. Al-Khidr, known in the Qur'an as the Green One, showed Moses paradise to be a turquoise cage of birds. Sura 76, verse 21, of Al-Insan states, "Upon them will be green garments of fine silk and heavy brocade, and they will be adorned with bracelets of silver; and their Lord will give to them to drink of a Water Pure and Holy." The bracelets on our wrists are inter-dimensional voices beamed from the Ophiuchus constellation. We stare at the map on the wall and see a trajectory out of THE LEVEL OF THE DEAD. Participant Y states that at about 1hr 3'00" the room was filled completely with mist and he saw the eyeball of OBIDOS appear inside a great marbled corridor. He walked through a vast castle in the northern courtyard of the walled city. Along the corridors were one hundred doors. OBIDOS waited for him in the hundredth room behind the hundredth door.

FIG N. THE EYEBALL OF OBIDOS BEHIND THE
HUNDREDTH DOOR

We sat in contemplative meditation for ten hours, navigating the quantum cadaver of Spinoza's God. As Artaud explains, "Not only are mortals rotten, the very atmosphere in which we live is materially and physically rotten, swarming with maggots, with obscene appearances, poisonous minds, and foul organisms." The central message of the Bible, from Lazarus through Christ Himself, is zombification because we are living inside THE LEVEL OF THE DEAD. Edom was a voodoo cemetery that Adam and Eve ran naked from: a bionic landscape of their deceased master. Vines of epileptic ganglia. Necrosis. The universe is a dead machine. OBIDOS dresses up the violet-bionic corpse in black satin for its cyber-programmed resurrection. Every night, we hijack the spinal cord of Ptolemy. Butterflies drenched in blue-white lymphocytes, rise from our hollow graves. A skeleton lowered into an iodine solution suddenly jolts into life.

At about 8 hrs 43'08", both myself and Participant Y began to rub the map of Ophiuchus in viridian dye. We saw the snake of Eden transform into a magneto-acoustic wave of homogenous plasma.

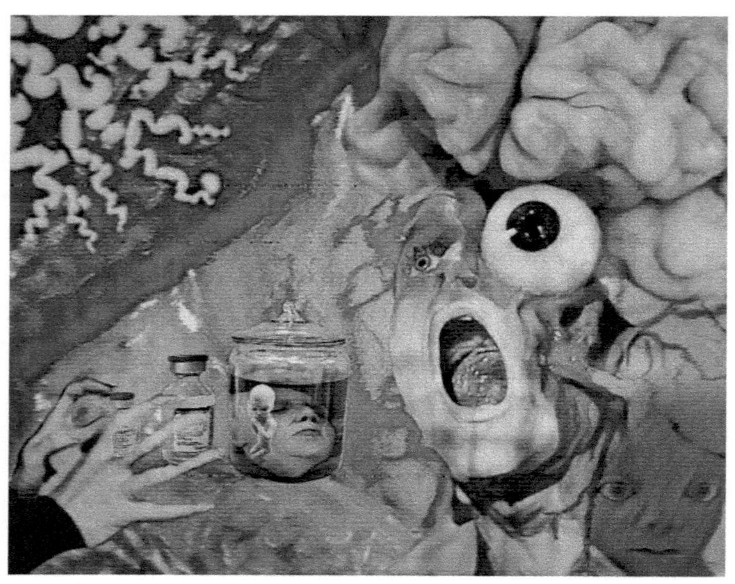

FIG O. PARIETAL CORTEX OF VIOLET-BIONIC-PTOLEMY

Cain and Abel each switched their transverse souls to follow their new destinies. We entered the walled city of OBIDOS, lost inside the jealous feathers of peacocks, Indonesian chickens riddled with vanity. They carry a red skeleton key in their beaks, beneath each doorway guarded by an alien keeper. The hundredth room in the northern palace is the home to Typhon—a viper-monster with one hundred hands. We kneel before its spheroid messenger that floats inside a courtyard covered in ivy and jasmine. We watch both suns rise in the southern skies.

A headless statue stands before a beautiful fountain. We see the bronze-green suns pause above the labyrinthine streets of OBIDOS. Our faces are pale and hollow. Our brains are fried. A priest anoints us in sacred cacti: green *psychotria*, yellow *myristica*, purple-furious *virola*. This city is the mind of OBIDOS. Paul the

Apostle ate dreaming flowers on his way to Damascus and saw a spaceship descend from a blank storm. He witnessed a UFO floating above the city of Ephesus. The Green One was an inter-dimensional being that showed Moses a viridian door inside his own head. We project ourselves along vectors of coaxial worlds into the sympathetic nervous system of our alien replicants. They look just like us. We greet them each night. Their eyes are open and clear. Goethe writes, "What is hardest of all? That which seems most simple: to see with your eyes what is before your eyes." The priest hands each replicant a single flower, a ghost orchid torn from the streets of Gomorrah. The light never ends. We are turning viridian. Our replicants are waiting in the darkness. The clouds begin to part in the window of the apartment. The street below is so still. It is time to see the world.

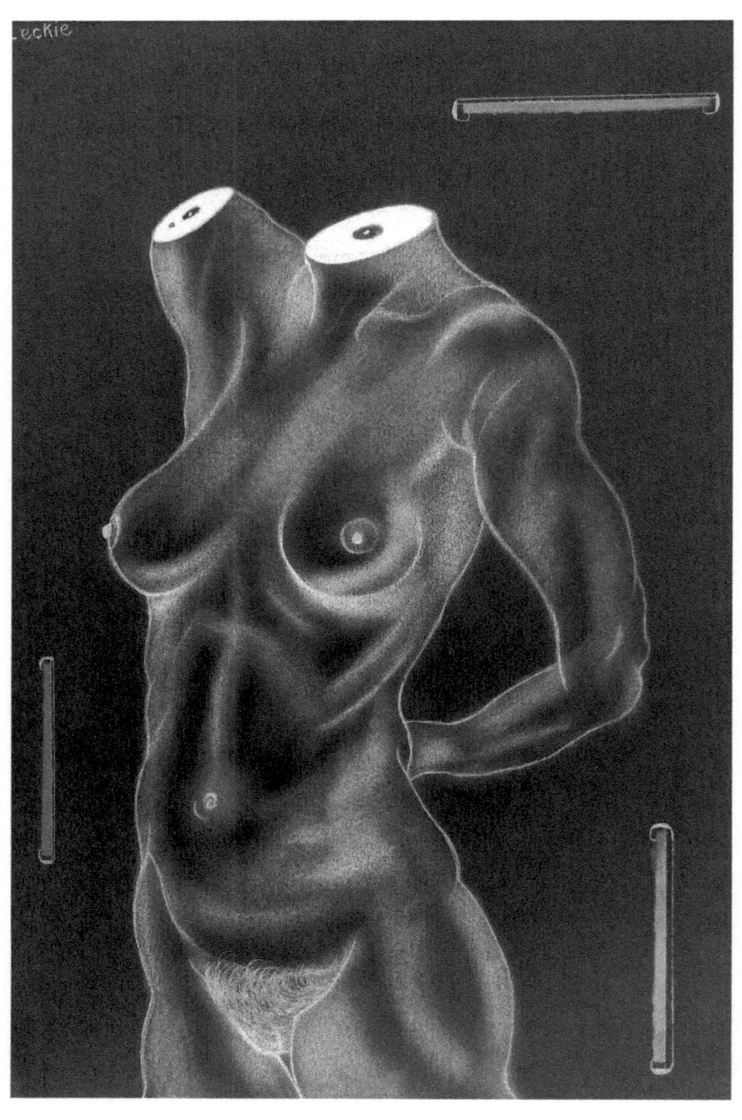

FIG P. STATUE IN NORTHERN COURTYARD OF OBIDOS

Internet - Stalling - Slow
Heavy Traffic - Comic
Puppees - Has proved
iE - by surpressing it
page UnResponsive
The Cosmic Puppees.
I saw God.
THEY Taszer
Bosomi
Tim + Ben
- nonce = Kimbo
04/08/16   +
Gold Light Jimbo
Paradise -   +
Heaven Hellsckco <s.
March 60 9gers = ?

ACKNOWLEDGEMENTS

Thanks to Elytron Frass who was involved in early discussions about these experiments. We would like to acknowledge his participation in our research of PSY-V-E.

The root is bitter. The leaves are deception.

LAY OUT YOUR UNREST